*Every new generation of children is enthralled by the famous stories in our Well-Loved Tales series. Younger ones love to have the story read to them, and to examine each tiny detail of the full colour illustrations. Older children will enjoy the exciting stories in an easy-to-read text.*

# The Princess
# and the Pea

retold for easy reading
by VERA SOUTHGATE M A B Com
illustrated by ROBERT AYTON

Ladybird Books Loughborough

Once upon a time, there was a prince. When he grew up he wanted to marry a princess. But he wanted her to be a *real* princess.

The prince went all over the
world looking for a *real* princess
whom he could marry.

The prince met many princesses but there was always something the matter with them. One was too tall and another was too small. One was too sad and another was too gay.

Somehow or other, not one of the princesses was just right. The prince was never quite sure if they were *real* princesses.

At last, the prince came home again. He was very sad because he did want to marry a *real* princess.

Then one night there was a terrible storm. The lightning flashed, the thunder roared, the wind blew and the rain poured down.

In the middle of the storm there was a knock on the door of the castle. The old king went to open the door.

There, standing outside in the pouring rain, was a lovely lady. She might have been a princess, but she was so wet that it was difficult to tell.

Her hair was so wet that the water from it was running down her face. Her clothes were so wet that the water was pouring out of them.

Her shoes were so wet that the water was running in at the toes and out at the heels.

The king led the princess into
the castle, out of the wind and the
rain.

There she stood, in a pool of water, and all she could say was, "I am a *real* princess."

The prince could not believe his
ears when he heard her say, "I am
a *real* princess."

The old queen heard her say,
"I am a *real* princess."

"We'll see about that," thought
the old queen, but she did not say
anything.

While the princess was being bathed and dried and dressed in dry clothes, the queen went to see about a bedroom for her.

The queen had all the bedclothes taken off the bed. Then she put a pea under the mattress.

Then more mattresses were put on top, until there were twenty mattresses on top of the pea.

Then the queen had many feather beds piled on top of the twenty mattresses.

"Now we shall find out if you are a real princess," said the queen to herself.

When the princess was warmed and fed, the queen led her to the bedroom and tucked her into bed.

In the morning, the old queen
went to see the princess. "How
did you sleep, my dear?" she
asked her.

"Dreadfully," replied the princess, "I hardly slept a wink all night!"

"What was the matter?" asked the old queen.

"I do not know what was in the bed," replied the princess, "but there was something hard in it. Now I am black and blue all over."

41

Then the queen knew that this was a *real* princess because she had felt the pea through twenty mattresses and many feather beds. Only a *real* princess could be as tender as that.

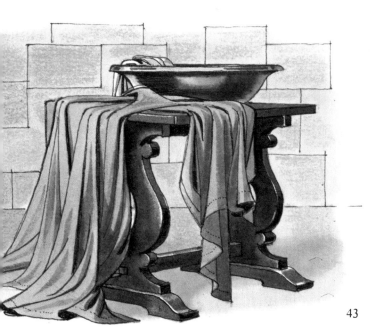

The prince was filled with joy
when the old queen told him that
they had indeed found a *real*
princess.

Now the queen had the pea
taken out of the bed so that the
poor princess could sleep well.

A wedding was arranged between the prince and the *real* princess. Then there was great joy in the castle.

As for the pea, it was placed in
a museum. It may still be seen
there—if no one has taken it away!